HIT A HOME RUN!

the TINY GENIUSES

1 FLY TO THE RESCUE!

2 SET THE STAGE!

3 HIT A HOME RUN!

READ THEM ALL!

the TiNY GENiUSES

HIT A HOME RuN!

by Megan E. Bryant

Scholastic Inc.

For Sam, a true Work of art.

Copyright © 2018 by Megan E. Bryant

All rights reserved. Published by Scholastic Inc., *Publishers since 1920*. SCHOLASTIC and associated logos are trademarks and/or registered trademarks of Scholastic Inc.

The publisher does not have any control over and does not assume any responsibility for author or third-party websites or their content.

While inspired by real events and historical characters, this is a work of fiction and does not claim to be historically accurate or portray factual events or relationships. Please keep in mind that references to actual persons, living or dead, business establishments, events, or locales may not be factually accurate, but rather fictionalized by the author.

ISBN 978-0-545-90963-1

10 9 8 7 6 5 4 3 2 1   18 19 20 21 22

Printed in the U.S.A.   40
First printing 2018

Book design by Maeve Norton

"Life is not a spectator sport."

—*Jackie Robinson*

"Feet, what do I need you for when
I have wings to fly?"

—*Frida Kahlo*

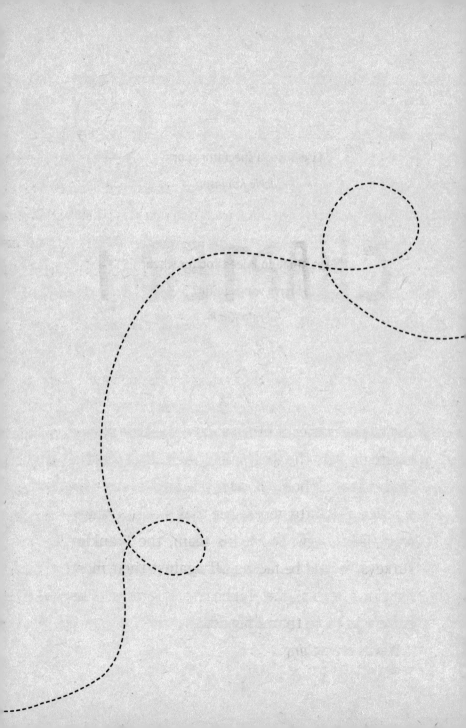

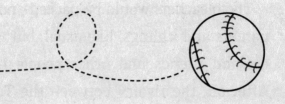

CHAPTER 1

Out of the corner of his eye, Jake Everdale stared longingly at the ball field behind Franklin Elementary School. It was deserted today—no practice this afternoon—but that would change soon, Jake knew. Soon, his team, the Franklin Turkeys, would be facing off against their most ferocious rivals, the Pinehurst Piranhas. The game was more than a big deal.

It was *everything*.

The bleachers would be packed—not just with parents and siblings, like usual, but with teachers and friends and other people from town. After all, the rivalry between the Turkeys and Piranhas stretched back decades. It had been a big deal when Jake's dad played for the Turkeys. Jake could imagine approaching home plate, the bat clenched in his fists . . . his eyes on the pitcher . . . the expectant silence of the crowd as they watched and waited, wondering—home run or strike out?

Thud!

Jake was jolted out of his daydream as someone shoved past him on the sidewalk, knocking him so hard that his backpack slipped off his shoulder and tumbled to the ground.

Jake didn't have to look. He already knew who had bumped into him.

"Way to walk, Everfail," Aiden Allen said, snickering as he loomed over Jake.

Ignore him, Jake told himself firmly. He knelt to pick up his bag and the stuff that had fallen out of it, hoping Aiden wouldn't notice his burning ears. Whenever Jake was embarrassed or angry, his ears always gave it away.

Luckily, Aiden strolled off, still chuckling to himself. Jake tried to relax, but his muscles were too tight. *If only Emerson hadn't left early for the dentist*, Jake thought. If he and Emerson had been walking together, Aiden probably wouldn't have bothered him.

Jake stopped suddenly, his hand hovering over his Thursday Packet.

There was a white envelope sticking out of it.

An envelope that said *Mr. and Mrs. Everdale.*

Jake swallowed hard. A letter home to his parents in the Thursday Packet was not good.

What did I do now? Jake wondered, racking his brain. He hadn't gotten in trouble, not even with the super-strict cafeteria lady who yelled at everybody. He hadn't failed any quizzes or tests . . . or forgotten to do his homework . . . In fact, fourth grade had been going pretty well, much to Jake's surprise. Usually by now, his teacher had sent a letter home asking for a conference because Jake "wasn't living up to his potential" or "had trouble paying attention in class." But this year was different. And Jake knew exactly why.

The old storm drain behind Franklin Field was legendary. According to the rumors, it was really a wishing well that would grant one wish to every student at Franklin—but only one. All you had to do was toss your most special belonging into the drain and make a wish. Jake had saved his wish since kindergarten, but when the fourth-grade science fair loomed, he knew it was finally time to use it. He hadn't wanted to part with his precious baseball card collection, though. It was *too* special. So Jake bent the rules a little and tossed in the Heroes of History action figures when he wished for extra help. He had never expected that the Wishing Well would bring them to life! First, brilliant scientist Sir Isaac Newton and legendary pilot Amelia Earhart helped him with his science project. Then Founding Father Benjamin Franklin and famous singer Ella Fitzgerald helped Jake with his big history presentation.

Jake realized he was still standing in the middle of the sidewalk, staring at the envelope to his parents. If only Jake could sneak a peek at the letter. Then he'd know how much he needed to worry. But the envelope was sealed.

With a sigh, Jake shoved the rest of his stuff in his backpack and finished walking home. His little sister, Julia, was sitting at the kitchen table dipping apple slices into peanut butter.

"Jake!" Julia cried. "I brought home so much good stuff in my Thursday Packet!"

"Great!" Jake said, trying to muster some enthusiasm. Thursday Packets in kindergarten *were* great, full of drawings and flyers for fun stuff in the community. Not mysterious sealed envelopes of doom.

"What's in yours?" Julia asked, trying to reach inside Jake's backpack. He twisted away from her.

"Cut it out!" Jake snapped.

Just then, Mom arrived with a bowl of pretzels. "Hi, Jake! How was your day?"

"Jake won't show me his Thursday Packet," Julia piped up.

"Can you *stop*?" Jake asked through gritted teeth. That was a mistake. Mom was instantly on alert.

"Whoa—what's the problem?" she said.

"I don't know," he said, and he handed Mom the envelope.

It only lasted for a moment, but Jake saw it: the flicker of worry that flashed through her eyes.

That made him feel even worse.

Mom didn't say anything as she opened the envelope. Her eyes moved back and forth while she read the letter. Then she looked up.

"Jake," she began, "do you know what this is about?"

"No," Jake replied, staring at the floor. "What?"

"It's a big field trip!" Mom exclaimed.

Jake blinked. *A field trip?* he thought. That was *not* what he expected.

"You're going to spend the entire day at the Museum of the World next Wednesday," Mom was saying, "for workshops and educational programming. And then your whole class will eat at Señor Taco's on the way home!"

Jake started to smile. Not just smile—*grin*.

"There's a contract here," she continued, "about behavior expectations. We'll review it with Dad after dinner. Then we all have to sign it."

"I wonder why Ms. Turner didn't say anything about the field trip at school," Jake said.

"Probably because it's such a big trip," Mom replied. "I appreciate that she told the parents before the kids could get all excited."

"Mom, can I use your phone to call Emerson?" Jake asked.

"You have five minutes," Mom said. "Then it's time to start your homework."

"Thanks!" Jake said. Then he charged up to his room, dialing on the stairs.

"Hello?" Mrs. Lewis answered.

"Hi! It's Jake. May I speak to Emerson?"

There was a pause.

"Hi, Jake," she replied. "His mouth is pretty sore. He can only talk for a couple minutes, okay?"

A moment later, Emerson's voice came onto the phone. "Whassup?" he said. It sounded like his mouth was stuffed with cotton balls.

"How did it go at the dentist?" Jake asked.

"Orthodontist," Emerson corrected him. "I got spacers between my teeth. It kind of feels like I caught a pop fly with my mouth."

Jake cringed in sympathy. Maybe hearing about the field trip would brighten Emerson's day. "Big news in the Thursday Packets," he said. "Guess what! We're going on a field trip to the Museum of the World!"

"What?" Emerson yelled. His voice was so loud that Jake imagined Emerson's mouth opening wide, and all those spacers between his teeth *sproing*ing out.

Jake told Emerson everything he knew about the field trip.

"This is going to be the best day of my life!" Emerson was yelling again.

"I know!" Jake replied. "I can't wait to try the Seven-Pound Burrito at Señor Taco's!"

"No, it's going to be even better than that," Emerson replied.

"What do you mean?" Jake asked.

Suddenly, Emerson got quiet. Too quiet.

"Tell you tomorrow," he mumbled into the phone. "I have to go. I have to . . . check something."

"Wait! Tell me now!" Jake begged. "Emerson? You there?"

But the phone was silent. Emerson had hung up.

Now Jake had no choice but to wait.

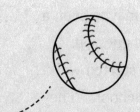

CHAPTER 2

The next morning, Jake got to Emerson's house earlier than usual for their walk to school. Jake wanted to ask all about the big secret from yesterday's phone call, but he remembered his manners just in time.

"How's your mouth?" Jake said.

Emerson smiled so that all his teeth showed. Jake could see some brightly colored bits stuck between them, as if Emerson had forgotten to brush his teeth for a month . . . or maybe even a year. "Are those your spacers?" Jake guessed.

Emerson nodded as he and Jake started walking toward Franklin Elementary School. "They don't really hurt anymore," he said. "But they feel pretty weird."

"Speaking of weird . . . why'd you act so weird on the phone?" Jake asked.

Emerson dug around in his pocket and pulled out a folded-up page from the newspaper. Now Jake was even more curious.

"Check *this* out," Emerson said as he handed the page to Jake.

Jake unfolded it carefully. At the bottom of the page was an ad that Emerson had circled about a hundred times.

BASEBALL'S GREATS

Hank Aaron · Jackie Robinson · Willie Mays · Babe Ruth

Mementos and Memories

Bats, Balls, Uniforms, and More! Never Before Available to the Public!

Limited Engagement · Two Weeks Only · Museum of the World

"Wow," Jake breathed. He looked at Emerson with wide eyes. "We *have* to go!"

"I know!" Emerson hollered excitedly. "And we are! Next week!"

Jake shook his head. "No—the field trip is for school," he reminded Emerson. "Mom says it's 'educational programming.' But we should definitely go to the baseball exhibit another time. Maybe my dad will take us."

"But the exhibit is gonna close," Emerson said.

"It's only at the museum for two weeks, and it started last weekend. I already asked my parents, but they're too busy."

"This is so depressing," Jake said. "I wish I didn't even know about it."

"Jake, Jake, Jake," Emerson said, shaking his head. "We are *literally* going to be right there. Yeah, sure, our class will be busy with—what did you call it?—educational programming? But the baseball stuff is in the *same building*. Do you get what I'm saying?"

Jake blinked. He sort of thought he understood, but at the same time, it was so unlike Emerson—he couldn't believe that *Emerson*, of all people, was actually suggesting—

"You think we should sneak away from our field trip . . . and go to the baseball exhibit?" Jake said slowly.

"Ding, ding, ding!" Emerson cried. "That's *exactly* what I think!"

"But . . ." Jake began.

"It will be so easy!" Emerson continued. "We

just kind of slip away from our group, check out the baseball stuff, then get back to our class. Nobody will even notice we're gone. There will probably be *thousands* of kids on field trips. We'll blend right in."

Jake didn't answer immediately. Emerson made it sound like it would be no big deal to sneak away during the field trip.

Could he possibly be right?

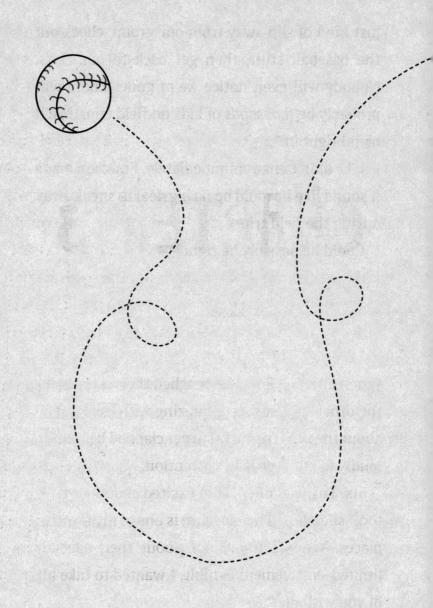

CHAPTER 3

When Jake and Emerson reached their classroom, the other students were buzzing with excitement about the field trip. Ms. Turner clapped her hands loudly to get everyone's attention.

Ms. Turner smiled. "I'm excited about our trip, too," she said. "The museum is one of my favorite places. When I found out about their special, limited-engagement exhibit, I wanted to take all of you with me."

Jake twisted around in his seat to look at Emerson. "Baseball?" he mouthed. Could it be possible that Jake's class was going to study his favorite game in the world?

"All eyes up here, please," Ms. Turner said evenly.

Jake immediately turned around to face front.

"'Five thousand years of art . . . in half a day!'" Ms. Turner read from the colorful brochure in her hands. "This is going to be an outstanding opportunity for us to learn a broad overview of art history. I hope when we return from our trip, you'll be inspired to learn more about different periods in art history and the artists who have brought so much to humanity with their talents."

So she wasn't talking about baseball, Jake realized.

"Hannah, Marco, would you pass out these handouts?" Ms. Turner asked. "I want to give you the art assignment now so you can be thinking about it while we're at the museum."

Since Jake was in the front row, he received one of the very first handouts. He scanned it and barely suppressed his groan. He had to choose a famous artist, learn all about him or her, *and* write a report? He should've known the museum field trip would come with a catch.

Jake shoved the assignment deep into his backpack. He wasn't going to worry about the artist report yet.

He didn't even want to think about it.

Jake spent the entire weekend not thinking about school—but every Sunday night, Mom and Dad made him get out his assignment calendar. Then Jake had to write down any tests, quizzes, or big projects coming up.

Which meant he had to at least look at the directions for the artist report.

With a sigh, Jake sat down at the desk in his room and dug around in his backpack until he found the handout. Two corners were stuck together with chewed-up gum, but Jake carefully peeled the edges apart and smoothed out the assignment as best he could.

GREAT ARTISTS: RESEARCH AND REPORT
FOR THIS ASSIGNMENT, YOU WILL WRITE A FIVE-PARAGRAPH REPORT ABOUT A GREAT ARTIST. YOUR REPORT SHOULD DISCUSS THE ARTIST'S LIFE AS WELL AS HIS OR HER WORK. WHAT INFLUENCED THE ARTIST? WERE THERE ANY EVENTS—IN THE WORLD OR IN HIS OR HER LIFE—THAT AFFECTED YOUR ARTIST'S WORK

TO CONCLUDE YOUR REPORT, PLEASE CHOOSE ONE OF YOUR ARTIST'S CREATIONS AND WRITE ABOUT HOW IT MAKES YOU FEEL.

Jake groaned. He was supposed to write about how a piece of art made him *feel*? He didn't feel anything about art.

The blank calendar loomed large in front of Jake. He'd have to start mapping out the stages of the project. When he'd pick an artist. When he'd start his research. When he'd start writing. *Ugh.* So many steps. So many things to remember. So much work—and the more he thought about it, the more overwhelmed Jake felt.

I don't have to figure this out right now, Jake thought frantically as beads of sweat dotted his forehead. *I'll—I'll tell Mom and Dad that I can't pick an artist until after the field trip. Isn't that the whole point of going to the museum? To see a bunch of paintings that will, like, inspire us?*

Jake stood up so fast his chair screeched across the floor. Downstairs, Mom and Dad were in the living room, watching a boring grown-up show.

"How's the weekly assignment calendar, champ?" Dad said.

Mom looked over at Jake. "Let's see it," she said, holding out her hand. But when Jake handed her the mostly blank calendar, her face fell a little. "This seems like a pretty light homework week," she said. "Do you have any new projects coming up?"

"Yeah," Jake replied. "A report about an artist. But I can't get started until after the field trip."

"Is that what the assignment says?" Dad asked.

"No," Jake admitted. "But I think the field trip will, um, inspire me and help me pick an artist . . ."

Jake's voice trailed off. It had made so much sense when he first thought of it. But now, in the living room, his words sounded like a lazy excuse.

"On the other hand," Mom began, and Jake could tell she was choosing her words carefully, "if you choose an artist *before* the trip, you can really focus during the exhibits."

"Great opportunities for research at the Museum of the World," Dad chimed in.

Mom got up and crossed the room to the book-shelf. "I know I have a book about art history around here somewhere," she said. "Unless I loaned it to Emerson's mom when she directed that play last summer."

"Maybe you could go to the library after school tomorrow," Dad suggested. "They'll have a whole section about art history."

"Can't. Practice," Jake replied automatically.

This time, Mom and Dad both looked at him.

"I mean, I can go before school," Jake quickly corrected himself. Of course Jake knew the rule by heart: schoolwork before baseball, always. But surely Mom and Dad didn't expect him to start skipping practices right before the big game against the Piranhas?

"Let me know if you find that book, Mom," Jake said. Then he trudged back upstairs. It was no use. He was going to have to get started on the artist report sooner rather than later. *And* he'd have to wake up extra early to start researching in the library if he didn't want to miss baseball practice.

But maybe there was another way.

Jake glanced over at Julia's dollhouse, which she'd loaned him after she found out about Sir Isaac. It was still in his room. Still waiting for another tiny genius to appear in a burst of magical sparks.

Should he do it?

Making a wish would be so easy. All Jake had to do was say the words. Of course, what came next was anything but easy . . . Jake knew all too well that the miniature action figures were hard to control, and it was even harder to predict what they'd do next. But the temptation was irresistible. One short sentence—just five little words—and maybe, if he was lucky, the Wishing Well would send him the artist for his report, just like it had sent him Benjamin Franklin for his history project.

No better way to learn about someone than to actually meet *them and ask them questions,* Jake thought, feeling even more tempted.

Maybe a miniature Monet . . . maybe a pint-sized Picasso . . .

Just do it, Jake told himself. He squeezed his eyes shut tight and whispered, "I wish for extra help."

POP!

CHAPTER 4

The sparks. The smoke. Jake's dog, Flapjack, howling anxiously outside the door. By now, Jake knew what to expect—including the sudden thrill when he realized that he was about to meet one of the most important people in history. He couldn't wait to discover who the Wishing Well had sent to help him with his art project.

The last thing he was expecting to see was a man wearing a baseball uniform.

the number 42 that caught Jake's eye ...st. Of course he knew number 42. Who *didn't* know number 42? The number for a ballplayer who was so great, they had retired it from Major League Baseball—forever. The number for a ballplayer who hadn't just piled up awards and honors; he had changed American history.

The man was crouched over, his hands on his knees, in a pose that Jake recognized. If Jake had to guess, he was on base—or he thought he was— and he was looking to steal the next one as soon as the smoke cleared.

Jake could help with that.

He took a deep breath and blew away the smoke. The ballplayer stood up and glanced around in surprise.

"That," he said, "is not home plate."

"Mr. Robinson?" Jake said. He could barely breathe. "Is that—is that really you?"

Jackie Robinson tipped his navy Brooklyn Dodgers cap with the "B" embroidered on the front. "Yes, son," he said. "Pleasure to meet you."

"I'm—I'm—I'm Jake. I—I—"

Mr. Robinson smiled understandingly as Jake stuttered. It was clear Jake wasn't the first person to be so awed by meeting Mr. Robinson that he had trouble talking. And no wonder. Before Jackie Robinson, baseball had been segregated because many white people thought that black people were inferior and should be kept separate. Jackie Robinson's talent, drive, and determination had proven them all wrong.

"Take your time," Mr. Robinson told him. "I'm not going anywhere . . . at least, not until the next pitch."

"I—I'll be right back," Jake said.

He dashed into the hall, closing the bedroom door behind him, and took a deep, shuddery breath. Jackie Robinson, one of baseball's all-time greatest heroes, was standing on his desk!

There was so much Jake wanted to ask him—so much he wanted to find out—but first, Jake knew he had to do something very important. If he didn't, Emerson would never forgive him.

He catapulted down the stairs, still breathless when he reached the living room. Mom looked up in alarm. "What's wrong?" she asked.

Be cool, Jake told himself. He'd never told his parents about the miniature geniuses, and he wasn't about to start now. It was bad enough that Julia knew about them.

"Nothing," Jake replied. "Just, can I use your phone? I have a homework question for Emerson."

Then inspiration struck.

"Actually, can Emerson come over for a few minutes?" Jake asked. "It would probably be easier if we looked at it together."

"On a Sunday night?" Mom asked, frowning.

"We just need ten minutes," Jake said.

"Make sure it's okay with Mrs. Lewis," Mom told Jake as she handed him her phone.

"Thanks!" Jake exclaimed, sounding way more excited about his "assignment" than he intended.

"This better be good," Emerson said when Jake opened the door just minutes after their phone call.

"Follow me," Jake replied.

Before they entered Jake's room, though, Jake paused and turned to Emerson. "Promise you won't freak out," he said. "And no yelling. Julia's already asleep."

Emerson rolled his eyes. "Freaking out is not my style," he replied. "But, fine, I promise."

"Okay," Jake said. "Prepare to have your mind blown!"

Jake wasn't sure what Mr. Robinson would be doing when they walked in. He realized—too late—that he had completely forgotten to give him the usual warnings about not leaving Jake's room or getting into anything dangerous. How long had he left him alone? Five minutes? Ten?

Luckily for Jake, Mr. Robinson was still on Jake's desk, exactly where he'd left him. Well, not *exactly*. Mr. Robinson was working hard to make something with sticky notes and paper clips. Jake squinted his eyes as he tried to get a closer look. Was it . . . maybe . . . yes! It was a miniature baseball diamond!

"Amazing," Jake breathed.

Just like Jake, Emerson had recognized Mr. Robinson the moment he spotted him. His eyes were huge, his mouth opened wide—

"Shh!" Jake reminded Emerson just in time.

"I can't believe it!" Emerson said in the loudest whisper Jake had ever heard. "The Wishing Well sent you Jackie Robinson? *The* Jackie Robinson?"

"I know, right?" Jake said. "I can't believe it, either! I was just sitting there, thinking about the field trip and the artist report and . . ."

When Jake's voice trailed off unexpectedly, Emerson tugged on his sleeve. "What? What were you going to say?" he asked.

"Maybe it's a sign," Jake whispered.

"A sign?" Emerson repeated.

"Yeah," Jake replied, growing more convinced with every word. "The Wishing Well sent Mr. Robinson as a sign that we should go to the baseball exhibit!"

It didn't seem possible, but Emerson's eyes went even wider. "Dude. Of course," he said. "Otherwise, Jackie Robinson makes no sense. This is it! The Wishing Well *wants* you to go to *Baseball's Greats*!"

Jake nodded his head toward the desk. "Want to meet him?" he asked.

"Are you *kidding*?" Emerson asked, his voice getting louder with every word. This time, Mr. Robinson looked up.

"Well, Jake, who's your friend?" Mr. Robinson asked.

"He knows I'm your friend!" Emerson yelled, forgetting Jake's warning.

"Keep it down," Jake reminded him. Then he turned to Mr. Robinson. "This is my best friend, Emerson. Emerson—this is Mr. Jackie Robinson."

Suddenly, there was a rustling sound in the doorway. Jake spun around to see Julia standing there, holding her stuffed bunny in one hand and dragging her blankie with the other. "What's going on?" she asked, her words garbled by a big yawn.

Jake shot Emerson a dirty look that said, *See what you've done?*

"Sorry," Emerson apologized. "I didn't mean to be so loud."

"I was *sleeping* and you *woke* me up," Julia said, her lower lip jutting out in a pout. She was always in a terrible mood when she was unexpectedly awakened. It was her lip, though, that really made Jake worry. When it started to quiver like that, it meant that Julia was about to start crying . . . and if she cried loudly enough that Mom heard her and came upstairs . . .

"Julia! Look!" Jake said urgently. "This is the one and only Mr. Jackie Robinson, one of base-ball's all-time greatest players!"

Jake watched Julia's face carefully. Nothing bored her more than baseball . . . but at the same time, nothing interested her more than the miniature figures that came to life when Jake needed extra help. Which emotion would win?

"Where did he come from?" Julia asked.

"I wished for extra help," Jake began.

POP!

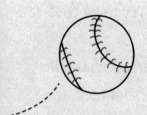

CHAPTER 5

No, no, no, Jake thought frantically as he waved his hands through the smoke. What had just happened? What had he said, exactly? He hadn't made another wish—at least, he hadn't *meant* to make another wish—

And yet, somehow, that was exactly what had happened.

Emerson opened and closed his mouth, but no words came out. "Did—" he finally managed to say.

"Yeah. I think so," Jake replied. "Try to be cool while we figure out who it is."

"Hank Aaron, Hank Aaron," Emerson chanted under his breath, crossing his fingers for luck.

"I want a queen!" Julia announced.

"Could you both zip it?" Jake asked. He didn't understand how the Wishing Well worked, but he was pretty sure it didn't take requests. And it seemed disrespectful to stand there placing orders while they waited for the newest genius to be revealed.

Through the haze, Jake could see a woman in a brilliantly colored outfit. She wore a full skirt, a ruffled blouse, and a fringed shawl. Her glossy black hair had been woven into thick braids that were topped with crimson flowers. The flowers matched the bold pattern in her skirt, which matched her bright lipstick. Every part of her outfit made the woman look like a work of art.

Then Jake noticed the bands around her arms. They were connected to long poles—and that's when he realized that the woman, whoever she was, was using old-fashioned crutches to keep her balance.

The woman locked her dark eyes with Jake's hazel ones. "*Que paso?* What happened?" she asked. Her precise English had an accent that Jake couldn't quite place. "This is not La Casa Azul. Where am I?"

Who are you? Jake wanted to ask—but he didn't want to be rude.

"I was painting and *whoosh*," the woman said with a graceful wave of her hand. "Where is my canvas? Where is my palette?"

"Um . . ." Jake wasn't sure what to say. "We can, maybe, help you get some . . . art supplies? But—could I—I mean, may I ask who you are?"

"You're her, aren't you?" Julia's small voice piped up as she peeked around Jake. Her eyes shone with wonder. "Are you Frida Kahlo?"

"I certainly am," the woman replied with a brisk nod of her head, making her gold earrings gleam.

Jake pulled Julia asde. "How did *you* know who she is?" he demanded in a low voice.

"Easy," Julia said with a shrug. "We learned about her in my art class. I can tell you all about her! She painted lots of pictures of herself, and she always wore the most beautiful clothes—"

"Thank you," Ms. Kahlo replied, smoothing her skirts. "This is a Tehuana dress, from the Tehuantepec region of Oaxaca."

"Where?" Jake asked, confused.

Ms. Kahlo pressed her hand to her chest. "Mexico," she explained. "My homeland. My heart."

"Ms. Kahlo," Jake began.

"Please, call me Señora Frida," she interrupted him.

Just then, Jake heard a noise. It wasn't coming from his desk.

It was coming from the door.

Everything seemed to happen in slow motion then, even though just a few seconds passed: the doorknob turning; the panicked glance that flashed between Emerson and Jake; the way Julia, of all people, dashed over to the desk and positioned herself *just right* to hide Mr. Robinson and Señora Frida from view.

Then the door opened all the way. Mom and

Mrs. Lewis stood in the doorway, with their best stern-mom looks.

There was complete and total silence.

"I don't know exactly what's going on in here, but I'm pretty sure it's not math homework," Mrs. Lewis said finally.

"Yes, Mom," Emerson said. "I mean, we're done with math. Sorry. Bye, Jake. See you tomorrow."

Suddenly, Mrs. Lewis's gaze landed on Jake's desk. Her eyes narrowed. "Is that—" she began.

Oh no, Jake thought frantically. Mrs. Lewis was pretty tall. Had she seen over Julia? And noticed the two tiny geniuses?

"A baseball diamond made of school supplies?" she asked.

"Come on, Mom!" Emerson hollered. "School day tomorrow! Need my sleep!"

He dashed out of the room so that Mrs. Lewis had to follow him—but not before she exchanged a knowing glance with Jake's mom.

"And as for you, young lady," Mom said with a pointed look at Julia, "it's back to bed."

Julia looked at Jake with panic in her eyes. He understood right away—if she moved, Mom would see Mr. Robinson and Señora Frida. And who knew what would happen next?

Then Jake had a brilliant idea. He sidled over to Julia and gave her a weird half hug to bump her off his desk so he could take her place—and block Mom from spotting the geniuses.

"Ow!" Julia howled. "I was *sitting* there!"

She turned to Jake with a scowl on her face—and then, to his surprise, gave him a great big wink.

"Oh, no. Don't start fighting now. It is *way* past your bedtime, Julia," Mom said firmly as she ushered Julia out the door. Then she paused. "And, Jake—was that really necessary?"

"Sorry," Jake said, his lips twitching with laughter. But he didn't dare laugh, or even breathe a sigh of relief, until Mom had closed the door behind her.

Jake turned to face Mr. Robinson and Señora Frida, who were watching with baffled amusement. "What was all that about?" Mr. Robinson asked.

"Sorry," Jake began. "It's just, Mr. Robinson, you're

one of Emerson's heroes. He's the only person I know who loves baseball as much as I do. In fact, we're about to go on this field trip to the Museum of the World, and there's a really special baseball exhibit—"

"Baseball? In a museum?" Mr. Robinson asked in surprise. "I sure would like to see that."

"You should come!" Jake said. The words were out of his mouth so fast that he barely realized what he'd done before it was too late. *What's wrong with you?* Jake asked himself. All his experiences had taught him that the tiny geniuses caused trouble wherever they went . . . even when they stayed in Jake's room.

But when Mr. Robinson, one of the greatest ballplayers of all time, showed interest in the baseball exhibit, Jake's response had been automatic. Of course he had to bring Mr. Robinson. How could he leave him behind?

"I'll come, too," Señora Frida announced.

"*You* love baseball?" Jake asked in surprise.

Señora Frida threw back her head and laughed. "I can't speak to baseball," she replied. "But I *do* love art."

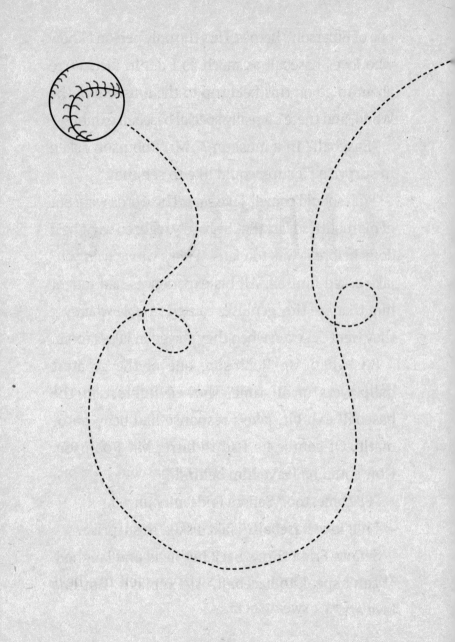

CHAPTER 6

On the morning of the field trip, Jake glanced warily at Julia's dollhouse. The trip, all by itself, would have been exciting enough. But combined with the plan to sneak into the baseball exhibit, and Mr. Robinson and Señora Frida's decision to tag along, Jake knew that the number of things that could go wrong was practically infinite. No wonder Jake's mouth was so dry he felt like he'd swallowed a sweat sock.

Jake's worries only increased as he walked to Emerson's house. "Do you remember the rules?" he asked Señora Frida and Mr. Robinson, who were tucked inside the secret pocket of his backpack. They may have been tiny, but they were still adults. It felt weird to tell them what to do. But Jake's experiences with the other tiny geniuses had proven that he couldn't be too careful.

"Stay in your backpack," Señora Frida replied.

"Stay out of sight," Mr. Robinson added.

"Absolutely, positively, no exploring on our own," they said at the same time.

"Good. Thank you," Jake said. He could see Emerson pacing on the sidewalk.

"Jake! My man!" Emerson hollered when he spotted Jake. "Are you ready for basically the best day of your life?"

"Listen," Jake began. "We—have company."

Emerson's eyes bugged out. "They came?" he asked.

Jake nodded. "When I told them about the trip—"

"That was your first mistake," Emerson interrupted.

Jake gave him a look. "Easy for you to say!" he replied. "You get to go home after we hang out. They, like, live in my room. I never get a break from worrying about what they'll do next."

"Sorry," Emerson said. "It's just, of course they wanted to come. Who wouldn't want to come? It's the Museum of the World! One of the coolest places in, well, the world!"

As the boys approached Franklin Elementary School, they saw two big school buses idling out front.

"Way-back seats, here we come!" Emerson cheered.

Emerson and Jake ran toward the nearest bus. A man they didn't recognize stood by the bus doors, holding a clipboard as he chatted with Principal Barron. Jake wondered if he was the bus driver, until he noticed that the man was wearing a neon-green Franklin Elementary School shirt with a colorful turkey on the front.

"Fourth-grade field trip? Step right up!" he announced when he spotted Jake and Emerson. "My name is Mr. Pelman. I'm the new guidance counselor."

"Oh! Hi!" Jake replied. "I'm Jake Everdale, and this is Emerson Lewis."

"Yesterday was my first day on the job," Mr. Pelman explained. "I thought I'd be unpacking my office today. But when Ms. Turner told me that one of the parent chaperones got sick, I volunteered to come on the trip. I love the Museum of the World. It's got everything!"

Emerson and Jake exchanged a smile. "That's what we've heard," Emerson said.

Mr. Pelman glanced at his clipboard. "You're both on bus number one, with me. Oh—one more thing . . ." He rummaged around in a box on the sidewalk. "Class T-shirts!" he announced. "Pretty snazzy, am I right?"

As Mr. Pelman held out a pair of neon-green shirts that matched his own, Jake hesitated for a second too long. "We—have to wear these on the trip?" he asked.

"You bet. School pride!" Mr. Pelman joked, posing with his chest puffed out. "They'll help us all stay together in the museum. It will be hard to get lost when you look like a firefly that fell into a nuclear power plant."

Jake and Emerson forced themselves to laugh as they took the shirts from Mr. Pelman. Then Emerson ran onto the bus to claim the way-back seat.

"Yes! All ours!" he cheered.

After the boys settled in, Jake peeked into his backpack. "You two okay?" he whispered.

"The air is pretty . . . close in here," Mr. Robinson told him. "Smells like a locker room after a doubleheader on the hottest day in August."

Jake glanced up quickly. "No one else is on the bus yet," he said. "You can come out for some fresh air. But just for a minute."

He held out his hand to help Señora Frida, then Mr. Robinson, climb to the top of the backpack.

"A bus?" Señora Frida asked. The corners of her mouth turned down in dismay. "I hate buses."

"How come?" Jake asked curiously. But she simply shook her head and stared out the window in silence. *Maybe Señora Frida was such a famous artist that she went everywhere in a limousine*, he thought. A school bus would be a pretty poor substitute for someone who was used to traveling in style.

Mr. Robinson was also frowning. "They're not *making* you sit back here, are they?" he asked Emerson.

"Make me?" Emerson asked. "No way. The back of the bus is the best. Jake and I always try to grab the back seat."

"It's like a private club," Jake explained. "Nobody can bug us or spy on us back here."

"You mean you *chose* the back?" Mr. Robinson asked in disbelief. "On purpose?"

"We got here extra early for first dibs," Emerson said proudly. "Anybody can sit anywhere they want, though. It's a free country."

"Well, I'll be," Mr. Robinson marveled. "You know, one time when I was in the army, the bus driver told me to move to the back of the bus, on account of my skin color. But I refused him. I planted myself in the middle of the bus, and I didn't budge."

"What did the bus driver do next?" Emerson asked.

The expression on Mr. Robinson's face was hard to describe—a mixture of pride and determination and resolve. "He had me arrested," he replied.

Jake's mouth dropped open. "*You?*" he exclaimed. "You were *arrested* for refusing to move to the back of the bus?"

"They were called Jim Crow laws," Emerson told Jake. "They were supposed to make black people feel like they were less than white people. And they were supposed to make them too scared to speak up or fight for their rights."

"Got myself court-martialed, too," Mr. Robinson added. "But I was found not guilty, and I received an honorable discharge from the army."

"I always thought it was Rosa Parks who refused to move to the back of the bus," Jake said, confused.

"Oh, she did," Mr. Robinson assured him. "Eleven years after I refused to move, Mrs. Parks did the same—and kicked off the civil rights movement."

"Were you angry?" Emerson asked. Jake wasn't sure if he was asking if Mr. Robinson was angry that Mrs. Parks was the one who was remembered for refusing to move . . . or angry about those awful Jim Crow laws. *Maybe both*, Jake thought.

Mr. Robinson chuckled. "In this world of ours, there's a lot to get angry about," he said. "You could spend every day of your life angry, if you wanted to. When I was a younger man, I wanted to fight every injustice, big and small. Now . . . well, now I know that sometimes the best way to take a stand against injustice doesn't involve fighting at all."

Jake was about to ask Mr. Robinson what he meant when Mr. Robinson cleared his throat and continued. "Anyway, things worked out fine for me, because it was just a few months after I got discharged from the army that I got the offer to play in the Negro leagues for the Kansas City Monarchs. Maybe my life would have taken a very different course if I hadn't gotten myself arrested on that bus."

"A bus ride seems like such an ordinary thing; a way to get from here to there," Señora Frida said, still staring out the window. "There's no way to know that it could change your life forever."

Just then, Jake heard voices. Clara and Hannah were climbing aboard, followed by Sebastian and—ugh—Aiden. "Quick—get down!" Jake whispered to Señora Frida and Mr. Robinson, who immediately disappeared into his backpack.

"Everfail! What are you doing here?" Aiden announced. "This trip is for *fourth graders.*"

Jake must've looked confused, because Aiden laughed loudly before he continued. "Didn't you get bounced back to third grade?"

Jake could feel his ears burning already. But he remembered what Mr. Robinson had just said—*you could spend every day of your life angry*—so instead of responding to Aiden, he turned to Emerson.

"What are we going to do about these Franklin Elementary T-shirts?" Jake asked in a low voice. "They practically glow."

"Yeah, I think that's the point," Emerson replied. "There's no way we can sneak off while wearing them."

"So . . ." Jake began, speaking even before he knew exactly what he wanted to say, "we'll just have to take them off."

"Are you serious?" asked Emerson.

"Just for a little while," Jake replied. "Just long enough to, you know, zip through the baseball exhibit. Then, boom! We'll put the shirts back on, get back to our group, and nobody will even know we were gone."

The engine rumbled as the bus pulled away from the curb. Jake instinctively reached for his backpack to keep it from sliding under the seat in front of him. A tremendous cheer rose up from the students as everyone realized, at the same time, that their field trip had officially begun.

"Next stop, Museum of the World!" Emerson announced.

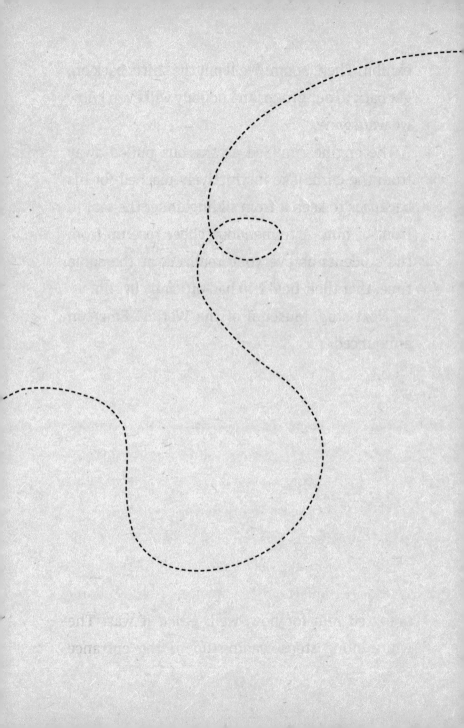

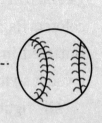

CHAPTER 7

An hour later, the bus erupted into cheers again as it arrived at the Museum of the World. "We're here!" Emerson hollered, bouncing up and down on the springy seat. "We're here!"

Jake, for once, was speechless. He stared out the window in awe. Jake had seen plenty of pictures of the Museum of the World, but they hadn't prepared him for how, well, *grand* it was. The white stone steps leading up to the entrance gleamed in the sunshine, while dozens of brightly colored flags from countries all over the world fluttered in the breeze. No wonder Ms. Turner loved it so much.

"All right, listen up, friends," Mr. Pelman announced. "I want everyone to put on your Franklin Elementary T-shirts before we get off the bus. Wear them with pride, Turkeys!"

Jake and Emerson exchanged a sly smile as they pulled on the neon shirts.

"Remember the contract you all signed," Mr. Pelman continued. "Buddy system, stick with the group, no roughhousing, no wandering. We're representing Franklin Elementary School."

Jake's smile faded as his conscience started to prickle. He tried to catch Emerson's eye again, but Emerson was chatting excitedly with Sam across the aisle. Mr. Pelman was right. They *had* signed a contract. If something went wrong . . . If they got caught . . .

Jake tried to push the thought from his mind. He and Emerson had planned their lightning-fast tour of the baseball exhibit down to the very last detail. Nothing would go wrong . . . as long as they stuck to the plan.

"Here we go." Mr. Pelman's voice boomed through the bus.

Jake and Emerson scrambled down the narrow aisle and joined the crowd of neon-wearing Franklin students.

Ms. Turner blew her whistle. "Follow me!" she called, leading the group up the massive stairs.

The lobby of the museum was filled with so many amazing artifacts that Jake would've been content to stand there and marvel at it all. Ancient banners hung from the rafters beside swooping pterodactyl skeletons that dangled from delicate wires. Tall pedestals throughout the lobby held everything from a rare orchid to a shining suit of armor.

Suddenly, Emerson grabbed Jake's arm and jerked it so hard that Jake nearly stumbled into him. Jake—cradling his backpack extra carefully—recovered his footing just in time to avoid a collision.

"Dude! Why—" Jake began. Then he realized that Emerson had pulled him into an alcove that was partially concealed by a velvet drape. In the shadows of the alcove, no one could see them. And if they were really lucky, no one would miss them, either.

"Quick—let's stash our shirts," Emerson whispered. "Then we can look at the map I printed last night."

"Good call," Jake replied. He shoved his neon turkey shirt to the very bottom of his backpack.

Emerson had folded the museum map into a tight, tiny square, like a perfect piece of origami. He spread it out on the floor and tried to smooth the creases with his hands.

"I think we're . . . right about here," Jake said as he studied the map, searching for the hidden alcove. "So the quickest way to the baseball exhibit is—"

"The elevators," Emerson interrupted. "Not the Space Lab ones, the ones by the Butterfly Pavilion."

"This escalator might be even closer," Jake pointed out.

"But first . . . *las mariposas, por favor?*"

At the sound of Señora Frida's voice, Jake jumped. She and Mr. Robinson had climbed out of his backpack—*that broken zipper!* Jake thought in frustration—and now they were studying the map, too.

"What did you say?" Jake asked.

"*Las mariposas.* The butterflies. They are right here, are they not?" Señora Frida continued. "It would be easy enough to step inside this— pavilion, is it?—to see them?"

"No way," Emerson began. "I mean, the Butterfly Pavilion isn't part of our plan. We don't have a lot of time to find the baseball stuff and get back to the group."

"Besides," Jake said, "the sooner we finish with baseball, the sooner we can check out all the awesome paintings! Doesn't that sound incredible?"

"The Butterfly Pavilion is just a fancy name for an overgrown garden," added Emerson. "It's full of fruit and flowers for the butterflies, and it's hot and humid . . ."

Señora Frida's eyes lit up. "A garden?" she cried. "I have the most glorious garden at La Casa Azul, filled with fruit trees and the plants of my homeland. Apricots and pomegranates! Agave and cactus!"

Jake and Emerson exchanged an anxious glance. "We don't—" Jake began.

But Señora Frida, beaming, was still talking. "There is so much inspiration to be found in nature. Birds and monkeys, fruits and flowers; I have painted them all. I will go to this garden, this pavilion of butterflies, and perhaps *las mariposas* will flutter into my next painting."

"Now, let's just hold on a minute," Mr. Robinson spoke up. "These boys have been talking about the baseball exhibit since I met them. We ought to—"

"*You* want to see the baseball; *I* want to see the butterflies," Señora Frida replied. "My painting is not less important than your passion."

"Nobody said that," Jake said helplessly. "But—"

"They are right here," Señora Frida said, tapping the map with her crutch. "*Con permiso*—"

Then, with bright colors flashing as her skirt swirled, Señora Frida ducked around the curtain.

"No! Stop!" Jake cried as loud as he dared. He turned to Emerson, frantic. "You've got to stop her—"

"No, *you've* got to stop her," Emerson argued. "I don't want to miss the baseball exhibit with Mr. Robinson!"

Jake ran his hands through his hair until it was all scrunched up. It wasn't his fault that Señora Frida had dashed off—but it wasn't Emerson's, either . . .

"Rock-paper-scissors," Jake said desperately. "One—two—three—"

Jake clenched his fist to make the rock sign. At the same time, Emerson made the scissors sign. He groaned when he realized he'd lost. "I *always* try to figure out what you're going to pick, and I *always* guess wrong," he said.

"Just go," Jake replied. "Meet us at baseball after you find her."

"Fine, whatever," Emerson said before he stormed off to follow Señora Frida.

"Wait!" Jake called suddenly. But it was too late. Just like Señora Frida, Emerson was gone.

Jake didn't know what to do. Had this whole plan been a terrible mistake? Now that he was on his own, without Emerson, Jake was even more anxious. What would happen if they got caught? *Maybe I should put on my shirt and get back to the group*, Jake thought anxiously. But he couldn't do that—he'd just told Emerson to meet him at the baseball exhibit. Plus, Jake didn't want to disappoint Mr. Robinson, who was just as eager to check out the baseball memorabilia as the boys were.

"Okay," Jake said, sighing as he held open his backpack. "Let's find the baseball exhibit."

But Mr. Robinson shook his head. "Don't stick me in that backpack again," he said. "I want to *see* the exhibit, not just hear everyone else talking about it."

"Nobody can see *you* when you're in the backpack, though," Jake said. "Don't you understand what a disaster it would be if someone noticed you?" He hoped that the urgency in his voice would convince Mr. Robinson. With the broken zipper on his backpack, though, Jake knew that Mr. Robinson could do whatever he wanted—whether or not Jake approved.

"Your pocket," Mr. Robinson said, pointing at Jake's chest. "How about I hitch a ride in there instead?"

Jake glanced at his shirt pocket, which was just Mr. Robinson's size. It even had a buttonhole where Mr. Robinson could peek out without being seen.

"Okay," Jake gave in. "But *please* stay out of sight."

Jake cautiously peered around the curtain before he crept out of the alcove. But all of his worries seemed to melt away as he approached the baseball exhibit. The doorway was decorated with vintage pennants and banners; as Jake stepped through it, he heard a scratchy recording from an old game. Jake could stand there and listen to it, play by play; if he closed his eyes, he could pretend he was really there.

But Jake didn't want to close his eyes, not even for a minute. There was way too much to see! Roberto Clemente's jersey. Joe DiMaggio's glove. Lou Gehrig's bat. Jake wanted to stop and stare at every item; he wanted to read every word on the cards mounted next to them. He could already tell that this exhibit wasn't just about baseball. It was about hopes and dreams. Disappointments and defeats. It was about the legends who had transformed baseball from a fun game into an American tradition.

Jake felt Mr. Robinson shifting in his pocket. "Can you see okay?" he asked under his breath.

"Kind of." Mr. Robinson's voice was muffled by the fabric of Jake's shirt, but that was just as well. The last thing Jake needed was for anyone to wonder why he was having a conversation with his pocket.

But the exhibit was so incredible that Jake just couldn't keep his mouth shut. "Oh, wow," he breathed. "I can't believe it!"

"What?" Mr. Robinson asked, squirming again.

"It's the last baseball pitched by Satchel Paige in the big leagues," Jake said in a whisper, starring at the scuffed ball atop a glass pedestal. "It's close enough I could touch it."

"Are you putting one on?" Mr. Robinson asked. "Satchel Paige might just be the greatest player of all time! He could've broken the color barrier, you know."

"Huh?" Jake asked.

But Mr. Robinson, staring at the ball, didn't seem to hear him. "I want a better look," he announced.

It took Jake a second to understand what Mr. Robinson meant. "No," Jake said, a little louder this time. "That's not possible. We're not allowed to cross that rope . . ."

But Mr. Robinson had already poked his head out of Jake's pocket. His face broke into an expression of awe.

What happened next happened so fast that, afterward, Jake would spend hours trying to remember exactly how it went down. Mr. Robinson hoisted himself out of Jake's pocket and scrambled up to Jake's shoulder. Then Mr. Robinson slid down Jake's sleeve and took a flying leap toward the pedestal!

"Stop!" Jake tried to say.

But the word got stuck in his throat.

The edges of Jake's vision went blurry as he focused with laser intensity on Mr. Robinson, dashing and darting toward the pedestal. There were dozens of people nearby, and all it would take was one, just one, to notice the tiny figure that was actually, impossibly, approaching Satchel Paige's baseball.

Jake acted on pure instinct.

He lunged forward with his hand out. If he could just pick up Mr. Robinson . . . It wouldn't be hard, not nearly as hard as catching a pop fly with the sun shining right in his eyes . . .

The rope.

In his panic, Jake had forgotten about the rope.

It was like a red-velvet boa constrictor that snaked around his ankle. Jake did a ridiculous twist-hop move that immediately attracted more attention than just about anything Mr. Robinson could've done. Trying to free himself only left him more tangled . . . and dangerously off-balance . . .

By the time Jake realized that he was going to fall, there was nothing he could do to stop it.

He couldn't even angle himself *away* from Satchel Paige's famous baseball.

Jake squeezed his eyes shut as his shoulder slammed into the glass pedestal. Everything was wobbling—the pedestal and the baseball and especially Jake—

Then they all tumbled to the floor at the same time, in a spectacular thud and crash of breaking glass.

WHEET! WHEET! WHEET!

When the alarm began to blare, Jake's eyes popped open in horror. He was vaguely aware of a rustling in his pocket as Mr. Robinson scurried back to his hiding place. Jake glanced around frantically—everyone was looking at him. In some distant part of his brain, Jake knew that he was about to be in the biggest trouble of his life—

Then he noticed Emerson and Señora Frida standing in the doorway, staring at him in shock.

"Get out of here!" Jake tried to tell them, but he doubted they could hear him over the ear-splitting alarm. Jake's heart felt like it was pulsing in time to the alarm's shrieks. He shut his eyes again, wishing he could go back in time and undo every single choice he'd made since he got off the bus.

Then strong arms were lifting Jake up and pulling him away from the destroyed display. Jake knew he'd have to open his eyes and face what he'd done—and the mountain of punishments that were surely in store.

But when Jake tried to put weight on his ankle, it wobbled worse than the pedestal. He cried out, as a sharp pain jolted through the joint.

"Steady now," a deep voice said.

As a pair of hands grabbed Jake's shoulders, he finally found the courage to open his eyes.

And stare straight into the stone-serious face of a security guard!

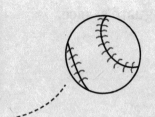

CHAPTER 8

"Where are your parents?" the guard demanded.

Jake swallowed hard and glanced back toward the door. Part of him was glad to see that Emerson and Señora Frida had disappeared—he didn't want Emerson to get into trouble, too—but he would've given anything to see a familiar face at that moment.

"I—uh—um . . ." he stammered.

A knowing look crossed the guard's face. "School group?" he barked.

Jake nodded miserably.

"Which school?"

"Franklin Elementary," Jake mumbled.

The guard held a walkie-talkie near his mouth. "We got a student separated from his group," he announced. "Page Franklin Elementary and send janitorial to *Baseball's Greats*. Also a curator. I've secured the artifact, but you know how they get when an exhibit has been tampered with."

Just when Jake thought he couldn't feel any worse, he heard the announcement echo throughout the entire museum: "Would an adult from Franklin Elementary School please come to the *Baseball's Greats* exhibit at once?"

Then: "Janitorial and Curation, please report to *Baseball's Greats*."

Jake squeezed his eyes shut tight, but a single tear slipped down his cheek anyway. At first, he thought it was embarrassment, but then he realized that the stabbing pain in his ankle was getting worse by the second. He tried to stretch out his foot, but the sharp pain made him gasp.

"You hurt yourself?" the guard asked.

"M-maybe," Jake said with a loud sniff.

"Let's get you over to the bench," the guard replied. He helped Jake limp over to a bench by the wall, where Jake waited for a chaperone from his school to arrive. Who would it be? Ms. Turner? Mr. Pelman? One of the parents? Jake wished he didn't have to see any of them.

But unlike so many of his other wishes lately, that one didn't come true. Ms. Turner practically flew into the room, a look of panic on her face. When she saw Jake on the bench—and the shattered glass, glittering under the exhibit's bright lights—the panic changed to confusion— then worry—

Jake knew what was coming next. Anger.

"Jake! What happened?" she exclaimed.

"I . . ." Jake said, too ashamed to find the words. But he knew that he'd have to tell her everything.

Well . . . almost everything.

"I—I—I wanted to see the baseball exhibit," he continued. "I—snuck away from the group. But I . . . got too close and got tangled in the rope . . . and tripped into the case holding Satchel Paige's ball."

Did the faintest hint of a smile flicker across Ms. Turner's face? It must've been Jake's imagination, because her mouth immediately fell into the sternest, maddest frown he'd ever seen.

"I hurt my ankle," Jake said. "It's hard to walk."

For a long, agonizing moment, Ms. Turner didn't say a word. She pulled down Jake's sock to reveal his ankle, which was already as red and swollen as an apple.

Ms. Turner sucked in her breath. Then she reached into her purse.

"Jake," she began. "I'm calling your parents."

A few hours later, Jake was lying on his bed with a bag of frozen peas wrapped around his bandaged ankle. He had never been more miserable in his life—and the throbbing pain wasn't even the worst part. He couldn't stop thinking about how much he'd messed up and how many people he'd disappointed. Ms. Turner, Mom, Dad . . . not to mention Emerson! Jake had blown Emerson's chance to see the baseball exhibit. Would Emerson ever forgive him? And Emerson had been responsible for Señora Frida all by himself, for the entire day. What if something had gone wrong and she'd gotten lost?

At least Mr. Robinson had come home safely, but Jake was too upset to watch him running drills around his desk.

Then there was a tap at the door.

Jake's stomach clenched. Mom was waiting for Dad to come home—this was definitely a two-parent lecture kind of offense—and Jake had been dreading it since they left the museum. "Come in," he croaked as Mr. Robinson froze.

When the door opened, though, it was Emerson. Mr. Robinson waved as he started running drills again.

Emerson's worried eyes looked from the

crutches propped against the wall to the bandage on Jake's foot to the peas on his ankle. "Are you okay?" He gasped.

"It's just a sprain," Jake replied. "It looks worse than it is. And feels worse, too, I guess. The doctor said I'll have to use crutches for the next couple weeks."

"But—you can't miss two weeks of practice!" Emerson exclaimed. "How are you gonna play on crutches?"

Jake gave him a look. "You're kidding, right?" he asked glumly. "After what happened at the Museum of the World, I'll be lucky if—"

Jake swallowed hard as the words caught in his throat. He couldn't even finish the sentence: *I'll be lucky if they ever let me play for the Franklin Turkeys again.*

Luckily, Emerson seemed to understand the seriousness of the situation. "This is all my fault," he groaned, burying his head in his hands. "It was *my* dumb idea. What was I thinking?"

"What was either one of us thinking?" Jake asked, shaking his head. "Anyway, how was the rest of the trip?"

"Nobody could stop talking about you," Emerson said. "They're all dying to find out what happened."

"What did you tell them?"

"Nothing," Emerson said firmly. "If I told anybody anything, I'd probably get into trouble, too. Besides, it's not like I knew that much. When Señora Frida and I got to the baseball exhibit, you were already crashing into—"

"Don't remind me," Jake interrupted Emerson as his ears started to burn.

"Sorry," Emerson said. "Anyway, all they knew was that an alarm went off, and Ms. Turner got paged, and you had, like, vanished, and when Ms. Turner got back, she was really grumpy for the rest of the day. Aiden told everybody you tried to steal something."

"I wouldn't do that!" Jake exclaimed. He sighed.

"Where's Señora Frida? Please tell me she's safe with you."

"Right! That's why I'm here," Emerson said. "Well, one reason anyway." He helped Señora Frida out of his backpack and brought her over to Julia's dollhouse. "She was *not* impressed by the Seven-Pound Burrito I ordered," Emerson told Jake under his breath. "I guess the food at Señor Taco isn't that authentic."

"Americans!" Señora Frida exclaimed with an amused smile. "I have always enjoyed my visits to your country, but please, explain to me why you think bigger is always better. In Mexico, you would not serve a Seven-Pound Burrito. What would be the point? The flavor of the spices and the freshness of the masa harina are powerful enough on their own."

Then she disappeared into the dollhouse.

"Oh, and, Jake?" Emerson said. "There was one more thing that happened today."

"What?" asked Jake.

"There was an extra part of the art assignment

that we did at the museum," Emerson replied. "We have to paint an original picture in the same style as the artist for our report. The museum's art teachers helped us get started. I told Ms. Turner you wanted to do Frida Kahlo . . . because of Señora Frida and all . . . I hope that's okay."

"Whatever. I don't care," Jake said as he flopped back and pulled a pillow over his face. Just when he thought his day couldn't get worse, here was news about *another* assignment that he was sure to fail.

"Check it out," Emerson continued. "Mom took me to the art store and we got all the stuff you'll need. There's a canvas and a bunch of paints— the good kind, not the kid stuff. I even got the smallest paintbrush they had for Señora Frida. The handle's too long, but if you break it in half she could probably use it. And I found your mom's book on famous artists, too."

"Thanks," Jake mumbled into his pillow.

There was a long silence.

"Well, uh, I'm sure Ms. Turner will tell you about it," Emerson finally said.

"Yeah," Jake replied. "Mom and I have a meeting with her and Mr. Pelman tomorrow. That's probably when they're gonna tell me that I'm getting expelled from school."

Emerson's eyes widened with worry. "Do you really think that might happen?" he asked.

"I have no idea," Jake said. He thought about returning to Ms. Turner's class, where everyone would be whispering about him like he wasn't even there. Not to mention how much Aiden would enjoy every minute of it. "But at this point, it might be an improvement."

CHAPTER 9

Jake didn't get much rest that night. Every time he moved in his sleep, his throbbing ankle awoke him. Even worse, though, was the doom he felt knowing that every passing minute brought him closer to meeting with Ms. Turner and Mr. Pelman. Jake had never dreaded anything more.

Just before dawn, Jake woke again. He could hear Flapjack barking outside. *That's weird*, he thought. Mom and Dad never let Flapjack outside that early.

That was when Jake realized that something very unusual was going on.

He bolted upright, his heart hammering in his chest. "Mr. Robinson?" he whispered as loudly as he dared. "Señora Frida?"

There was no answer.

Jake tried again, louder this time. "Mr. Robinson! Señora Frida!"

But all he could hear was Flapjack's distant bark. *He'll wake up the neighbors*, Jake fretted. *He'll wake up Mom and Dad!*

Jake swung his legs over the bed and peeked inside Julia's dollhouse.

It was empty!

And that's when Jake noticed that his bedroom door, which he had closed so carefully last night, was open. Just a few inches—but wide enough for a pair of action figures to escape from his room. There was no doubt about it now: Señora Frida and Mr. Robinson were on the loose!

Jake reached for his crutches and hobbled to the door, trying to come up with a plan. He'd get downstairs and put Flapjack in the mudroom; hopefully that would buy him a little time before Mom and Dad got up. Then he'd search the whole house, from top to bottom. Maybe he'd even wake up Julia so she could help.

Jake's nose twitched. What was that smell? It smelled kind of good—onions and garlic and something spicy that tickled his nose—but also kind of burned—

Oh no! Jake thought, and tried to go even faster.

It turned out that Mr. Robinson and Señora Frida weren't hard to find after all. The kitchen blazed with light, which shone through a dense haze around the stove—

The stove! Jake thought, in such a panic that he didn't notice the slimy trail of broken eggs across the kitchen floor. One pan held a pair of sizzling eggs; another held corn tortillas that were starting to brown. Then there was a pot full of some kind of tomatoey sauce, and another one filled with . . . beans? One of the pans was definitely smoking. Or was it *all* of them?

"Jake! Up here!"

Mr. Robinson and Señora Frida, perched on the shelf over the stove, waved to get Jake's attention. They had tied one of Jake's shoelaces to a spatula and were attempting to lower it to the stove—that sizzling, smoking, *burning* stove—

"What are you doing?" Jake exploded.

"Trying to turn these eggs," Mr. Robinson. "I'll be honest, it's harder than it looks. But I bet you could manage it just fine."

"No, I'm not talking about the eggs—I mean, I am, but what *is* all of this?" Jake asked.

"Well, Jake, we felt responsible for your predicament and all," Mr. Robinson said, gesturing to Jake's crutches. "If we hadn't argued at the museum and been so determined to experience it for ourselves—"

"We want to make right by you, Jake," Señora Frida announced. "Emerson told me how eager you were for the meal at Señor Taco's—which, trust me, you missed nothing—"

"Uh—" Jake began, glancing frantically at the ceiling. Had he heard something upstairs? Footsteps, perhaps?

"Go ahead, Frida," Mr. Robinson encouraged her.

"So I told my friend Jackie here that we should make you breakfast," Señora Frida continued. "Something delicious from my country! Something *traditional*! And so we have . . . huevos rancheros! Ranchers' eggs! The food of the people is good enough for anyone!"

"We've got some crispy tortillas," Mr. Robinson said, "and Frida says the beans go on the side and the eggs go on *top*, with this salsa over the whites . . . now, mind, it's extra spicy, because I accidentally knocked a whole bottle of hot sauce in it . . ."

"It is not exactly authentic, but we did the best with what we've got," Señora Frida added.

Thump. Thump. Thump.

There was no mistaking the sound of footsteps overhead. Mom—or Dad—or both—were awake. Flapjack had spotted Jake through the window and was barking even louder now, demanding to be let in.

"This is really bad," Jake fretted. "Really bad!"

"I *beg* your *pardon*!" Señora Frida said, highly offended.

"Not the food," Jake said. "The—"

He had no time to think of a plan, or an excuse, or anything. He only had time to put Mom's apron on over his pajamas, then place Señora Frida and Mr. Robinson into the apron pocket. Their spatula clattered to the stovetop, Jake's shoelace trailing through the salsa.

And that's exactly how Mom and Dad found Jake: standing at the stove, apron-clad, splattered with super-spicy salsa as the smoke thickened.

"Jacob Everdale!" Dad yelled. "What is going on here?"

"I can explain," Jake said—though he really couldn't.

"Are you *cooking* without an *adult*?" Mom cried. "Why is Flapjack outside? Is that *smoke*?"

Mom rushed toward the stove, slipping and sliding through the raw eggs on the floor. In a flash, she turned off the burners and tried to wave away the smoke. Dad hurried to let Flapjack in, who promptly started slurping up the eggs.

Mom grabbed the spatula and pointed it at Jake, accidentally flicking salsa off the shoelace. "Explain yourself," she ordered.

"I . . . uh . . . wanted to cook you breakfast," Jake said. "To make up for what happened yesterday. It's . . . rangers' eggs."

"*Ranchers'!*" Señora Frida piped up from the apron pocket.

Jake pretended to cough. "Ranchers' eggs," he corrected himself. "It's, um, a traditional Mexican dish."

"I—I—I—" Mom sputtered. Jake had only seen her like this—too angry to speak—once or twice.

Luckily, Dad stepped in. "Best of intentions, champ," he began. "But you know better than this. You can't use the stove without an adult. No matter what!"

Jake ducked his head. "I know," he said. "I'm sorry. I'm so sorry, about everything. I don't know what's wrong with me. It's like I can't stop making mistakes."

When Mom sighed, it was like all the anger drained out of her. "Just . . . *think* before you act," she told him. "Try to consider the consequences of your actions before you do anything."

"I will," Jake promised.

"Besides, you need to stay off that foot," Mom continued. "If you want eggs, I'll make you eggs. Apron, please."

Pure panic made Jake's stomach lurch. How could he give Mom her apron with Señora Frida and Mr. Robinson in the pocket? But as Mom stood there, holding out her hand, he realized that he didn't have a choice.

When Mom pulled on her apron, a look of confusion crossed her face. "What's this?" she asked as she reached into the pocket.

Jake couldn't move. He couldn't even speak. Luckily, Señora Frida and Mr. Robinson had the good sense to freeze, even as Mom dropped them on the table with a loud *thud*.

A few hours later, Mom and Jake approached Mr. Pelman's office for their meeting. Jake's palms were so sweaty that they kept slipping off the grip of the crutches.

"Good morning, Mrs. Everdale, Jake," Mr. Pelman said. He gestured to a set of open chairs next to one already filled by Ms. Turner. "Please come in—and excuse the mess. I haven't finished unpacking."

"No need to apologize," Mom replied. "I'm sure you didn't expect to be dealing with a situation like this during your first week."

"You'd be surprised," Mr. Pelman said. "My job is never boring—ever."

Jake stared at the brass nameplate on Mr. Pelman's desk, which read NATHAN PELMAN, SCHOOL COUNSELOR. It was surrounded by cool-looking gadgets that Jake impulsively wanted to touch.

"Fidgeters," Mr. Pelman said.

Jake looked up.

"That's my collection of fidgeters," Mr. Pelman explained. "I like to have something to do with my hands. Sometimes kids do, too."

When Mr. Pelman nodded encouragingly at Jake, he took a chain with different sized rings attached to it. The metal was cool and smooth in his hands and, Jake realized, strangely calming.

"Shall we begin?" Ms. Turner asked.

Jake raised his hand.

"Yes, Jake?" Ms. Turner said.

"I just want to say—I'm really sorry," he began. "I know I broke a bunch of rules . . . and the contract I signed. I don't have a good excuse for what I did. I feel awful about it."

Ms. Turner and Mr. Pelman exchanged a glance.

"We appreciate that, Jake," Ms. Turner said. "But what happened was very serious. You put yourself—and your classmates—at great risk."

Jake scrunched down in his chair. He wished that he could shrink himself, smaller and smaller until he was the size of the tiny geniuses . . . or maybe even smaller.

"I've thought a lot about what happened yesterday," Ms. Turner continued. "And I'm not sure if I'm more surprised, or more disappointed. Sneaking away from the group . . . breaking your contract . . . that behavior is so unlike you, Jake."

Jake wished she would yell. It was almost worse to hear Ms. Turner says those things in such a calm, quiet voice.

"And, as the contract clearly says, there will be consequences for any breach of the rules," Mr. Pelman added.

"I understand," Jake said. "I deserve it."

"Jake knows that he has to accept the consequences of his actions," Mom spoke up. "He's also going to be punished at home."

Ms. Turner placed a piece of paper on the desk in front of Jake. "We've discussed this situation with Mr. Barron, and these are the consequences we've decided on."

"The principal knows?" Jake asked in surprise.

"Of course he knows," Ms. Turner replied. "This was a very serious infraction of the rules, Jake."

"We've also spoken with Coach Carlson," Mr. Pelham added.

That's when Jake knew it was going to be even worse than he'd expected. *They're kicking me off the team*, he thought numbly.

"Of course, you'll need to make up the work you missed at the Museum of the World," Ms. Turner said. "And write a letter of apology to your classmates for disrupting their field trip."

Here it comes, Jake thought.

"And you're going to be benched for the next three weeks," Mr. Pelman said. "You'll be expected to attend all practices as usual, though, to support the team."

It took Jake a moment to understand. "So you're not—I'm still on the team?"

"Yes—but you'll be on probation," Ms. Turner corrected him. "For the rest of the season. If you step out of line one more time . . ."

Ms. Turner didn't need to finish her sentence. The consequences were crystal clear.

"I understand," Jake said quickly. "And I'm sorry. Really, really sorry."

When Mr. Pelman and Ms. Turner stood up, Jake realized the meeting was over—and, amazingly, he had survived it.

Now he just had to survive the rest of the school day.

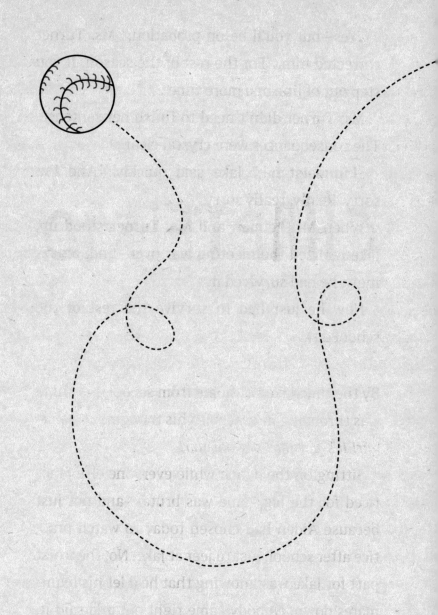

CHAPTER 10

By the time Jake got home from school, his ankle was throbbing in time with his thoughts: *It's-not-fair! It's-not-fair! It's-not-fair!*

Sitting on the bench while everyone else practiced for the big game was brutal—and not just because Aiden had chosen today to watch practice after school, just to jeer at Jake. No, the worst part for Jake was knowing that he'd let his teammates down. Nobody came right out and said it, but he could tell from the way they all got weirdly quiet around him. He was part of the team, but getting himself benched wasn't really acting like it.

Then there was the part that Jake didn't even want to admit to himself: how much it stung to see Emerson on the field, practicing with the rest of the team. Emerson had broken the rules, too. How come he didn't have to limp around with a sprained ankle? How come he wasn't benched for three weeks?

Jake slammed into his room, threw his crutches to the floor, and flopped facedown onto his bed. "Ow," he said, his voice muffled by his pillow.

"Does your ankle hurt?" a voice asked.

Jake rolled over. He hadn't noticed that Julia was in his room, messing around with her dollhouse. He also hadn't noticed that one of Mom's houseplants was turned over on his desk, spilling out soil that Mr. Robinson was using for his baseball field.

Jake focused all his frustration on Julia. "Why are you in here?" he demanded. "You're not supposed to be in my room without permission."

Julia pointed at Señora Frida. "*She* said I could," Julia retorted. "I'm *helping* her."

"Helping with what?" Jake asked rudely.

"Ta-da! La Casa Azul!" Julia exclaimed, spinning the dollhouse around on its platform. Jake flinched as something wet sprayed his face. He rubbed his hand across his eyes and was horrified to see blue streaks on his skin.

"What have you done with my paints?" Jake howled.

The back side of the pink plastic dollhouse was unrecognizable under a thick coat of blue acrylic paint. In her enthusiasm to show Jake, Julia's spinning of the dollhouse had splattered blue paint all over Jake's room—and all over his stuff!

"Well, we tried crayons, but they didn't work so good," Julia explained, pointing to a scribbly square of crayon graffiti on the side of her dollhouse.

"Emerson brought those paints for my artist project," Jake said through clenched teeth. Under ordinary circumstances, he would have lunged across the room to snatch all the supplies away from Julia, but with his sprained ankle, all he could do was limp.

"You're banned from my room! Forever!" he shouted as all his frustration and anger simmered to the surface and boiled over. "You don't help with the geniuses, you just make everything worse!"

An uncomfortable silence followed as everyone stared at Jake.

"Whoa, there," Mr. Robinson spoke up, his brow furrowed. "That's no way to talk, especially in front of the ladies."

Shame washed over Jake. He hadn't meant to lose his temper.

To everyone's surprise, Señora Frida threw back her head and laughed. "There is no need to worry about me," she announced. "I've seen people rage far worse. Come to think of it, I, myself, have raged far worse than poor Jake.

Señora Frida turned to Jake. "It was my idea to paint the house. La Casa Azul ... the Blue House ... just like my home in Mexico. That's where I do most of my painting," she said. "Since the accident. Of course, before the accident, I did not paint so much at all."

"What accident?" Jake asked.

"You did not know?" Señora Frida asked in surprise. She gestured to her crutches. "I was in a terrible bus accident when I was eighteen years old. It changed the course of my life. Before, you see, I was studying the sciences. I dreamed of being a doctor, of healing people in need."

A bus accident, Jake thought, remembering how unhappy Señora Frida had been on the bus to the museum.

"In one moment"—Señora Frida held up her hand and snapped loudly—"everything, everything changed. Good-bye to my dream of being a physician. Hello to my reality of being a patient. Surgery after surgery, month after month in bed, recovering, alone and adrift. There had to be some way to occupy the hours."

The silence deepened as everyone waited for Señora Frida to continue.

"And so I started to paint. I had a mirror installed on the ceiling so I could see myself while lying down in bed. That's who I spent most of my time with, you know, during those long and lonesome months. Myself. That's why I created so many self-portraits. Who did I know better to paint than myself, my struggles, my story?

"You have pain?" Señora Frida asked Jake. "Then you must use it. What else is it good for?"

"But—use it how?" Jake asked.

A smile crossed Señora Frida's face. "Only you can answer that question," she told him. "For me, the answer was art."

Jake still didn't understand. What exactly did

Señora Frida mean about using his pain? He was about to ask when she turned to Julia.

"All this talk, talk, talk," she was saying. "I have no more patience for it. Please, I should like to work on my painting now."

"Of course," Julia replied. She helped Señora Frida back into the dollhouse, where Jake spotted a small square of canvas stretched across four toothpicks: Señora Frida's painting in progress. He recognized the canvas; it had been cut from one of the storage bins in the playroom. *Mom's going to have some questions about how that happened,* he thought.

Back on Jake's desk, Mr. Robinson was whistling as he patted dirt from Mom's plant into a pitcher's mound. Now that Jake was calmer, he could marvel at Mr. Robinson's perfect miniature baseball field.

"You keep your cool no matter what, huh?" Jake asked him.

Mr. Robinson paused and looked up. "They didn't pick me to break the color barrier because I was the best, you know," he said.

Jake's face shifted into shock. "But—but you are the best," he stammered.

Mr. Robinson smiled as he shook his head. "I appreciate your enthusiasm, son, but I really wasn't," he replied. "Plenty of other players in the Negro leagues could've done what I did, and better, too."

Then . . . why you? Jake wanted to ask, but he didn't dare say the words out loud. It seemed almost disrespectful to think them.

"The truth is that the white men making the decisions—the men with all the power—knew that the player who broke the color line didn't just need the talent to do it, he needed the temperament, too," Mr. Robinson continued, as if he could read Jake's mind. "Who would keep his cool when his teammates snubbed him? Or when the fans jeered him? Or when the restaurants on the road wouldn't let him use the washroom, or the hotels wouldn't let him sleep under their roofs?"

A pained expression crossed Mr. Robinson's face. "But somebody had to be the first," he finally said. "And as hard as it was, I wouldn't change my mind about accepting their offer."

"Thanks, Mr. Robinson," Jake finally said when he found his voice.

"Anytime, son," Mr. Robinson replied. He picked up his bat and took a few practice swings.

Jake turned to the blank canvas.

Art, Jake thought. Señora Frida told him to turn his pain into art, which really didn't make much sense. How could he ever paint the swelling and throbbing of his ankle?

Or did she mean, like, emotions? Jake wondered. But how could Jake *paint* his feelings when he could barely talk about them?

Or was that the secret? When words failed, could paint succeed?

Jake flipped through Mom's art book until he reached the section on Frida Kahlo. There was a self-portrait of Señora Frida with a panther and a monkey and a necklace made of thorns; there was one where her heart was beating outside of her body. Jake's first impression of her paintings was that they were, well, weird—and normally he would have closed the book and moved on to something else. But knowing Señora Frida—knowing how passionate she was about her art, and knowing how the bus accident had changed her life—he couldn't help but look closer. *It's like her paintings are telling a story—but only part of the story,* Jake realized. Maybe Señora Frida was the only one in the world who would know the whole story. But looking at her paintings made Jake want to learn more.

Jake squirted blobs of paint onto the palette Emerson had brought him—blue and red, white and yellow. Or, to be more precise, Prussian blue and vermillion, titanium white and yellow ochre. The puddles of paint glistened, shiny and reflective.

Jake picked up the brush and started to paint.

CHAPTER 11

For the whole weekend, Jake worked on his painting, pausing only to use his best fort-making skills to string a sheet across the corner of his bedroom. He wanted to paint in private, without Mr. Robinson or Señora Frida or Julia watching.

On Sunday evening, Jake finally stood back. *Is it done?* he wondered. *Should I add more grass? Are the lines straight enough?* He soon realized that those were questions he couldn't answer.

But he could show it to someone . . . two special someones, actually. Jake knew he could trust them to tell him the truth.

Jake ducked his head around the sheet. "Um, Señora Frida? Mr. Robinson?" he asked tentatively. "Would you, uh, like to . . . well . . . see my painting?"

Mr. Robinson dropped his bat, but Señora Frida never let go of her paintbrush.

"Why, Jake, I'd be honored," Mr. Robinson told him.

"I thought you'd never ask!" Señora Frida added.

Feeling more embarrassed by the moment, Jake gave the sheet a hard tug. It fell to the ground, revealing his canvas. Jake stared at it anxiously. It didn't look the way he had pictured it in his mind—not even close, actually—but it wasn't terrible. You could tell it was a baseball field. The blobs of color in the bleachers definitely looked like a big crowd, if you squinted your eyes. And that little shape in the dugout, sitting on the bench—well, the average person might not know what that meant. But Jake did.

For a long moment, no one said anything.

"Well?" Jake finally asked. "What do you think?"

Señora Frida nodded her head. "Very nice, Jake," she said. "Very nice." She peered closer at the painting, and a small, secret smile crossed her face.

"I think it's fantastic!" Mr. Robinson exclaimed. "Just fantastic, Jake. Wow! If you play ball half as well as you paint—"

Jake had a feeling Mr. Robinson was exaggerating, but he couldn't help grinning. "Thanks, Mr. Robinson," he said.

"It just looks so real!" Mr. Robinson continued. He closed his eyes and breathed in deeply. "I can practically smell the dirt from the pitcher's mound . . . the fresh-mown grass . . . the roasted peanuts . . ."

Now Jake knew that Mr. Robinson was exaggerating. His painting definitely didn't look *that* real.

Señora Frida held up the tiny paintbrush that was still in her hand. "Jake—if I may?" she asked, gesturing toward the canvas.

"Um—sure," Jake replied in surprise.

"Just a small adjustment," Señora Frida said to herself.

"Looks like a real ball, even," Mr. Robinson marveled. "Like I could reach out and grab it—"

His hand moved toward the canvas at the same time Ms. Kahlo touched it with her brush.

"Wait," Jake started to say. "The paint's still—"

A sudden flash of light—

The sound of a crackling flame—

And just like that, Mr. Robinson and Señora Frida disappeared, right into the canvas that Jake had painted.

"Stop!" Jake cried. But it was too late—they were already inside his painting, made even smaller and yet somehow brighter and more vibrant. He couldn't hear a thing, but he thought he saw Señora Frida laughing with joy just before they vanished into the crowd, lost among all the people in the bleachers.

Jake sat back and exhaled a long, shuddery sigh. He wished he could've said good-bye—a proper good-bye—before the magic whisked them away.

Then again, there was no reason why he shouldn't try.

"Thank you," Jake said, not even feeling dumb for talking to a painting. "Thank you for everything."

Of course, no one answered. Jake didn't expect them to. But he kind of wished . . .

Jake smiled, shook his head, and stopped himself just in time.

The next morning, Jake's mom helped him bring his canvas to school. The artist project wasn't due for another week, but he wanted Ms. Turner to know he was serious about the assignment. He was serious about his make-up work, and serious about his punishment, and serious about earning back her trust.

It was early enough that none of the other kids were in class yet. Ms. Turner sat alone at her desk, grading a stack of quizzes. She looked up at the sound of Jake's crutches *thwack-thwack-thwack*ing on the tile floor.

"Good morning!" she said in surprise. "Is that your painting, Jake? Finished already?"

Jake nodded. "Once I got started, I didn't want to stop," he told her. It was true, too.

"Let's see," she said.

Mom leaned over to give Jake a hug. "I'll pick you up after practice," she whispered near his ear before she left.

Jake waited expectantly while Ms. Turner examined his painting. "Great job, Jake," she said. "I see Frida Kahlo—"

"Where?" Jake exclaimed, staring hard at the canvas.

"I see Frida Kahlo's *influence*," Ms. Turner continued with a smile. "There's a baseball diamond, sure, but also a celebration of nature—the bright blue sky; the rich green grass. It's like the dandelions and clovers in the field mirror the sun and the clouds in the sky."

Jake tilted his head as he stared at the canvas. He hadn't meant to do that, but now that Ms. Turner had pointed it out, Jake could see it, too.

"It's a beautiful day, yet there's a dark cloud overhead, too, casting a shadow over one small figure, apart from all the rest. Is that you?"

Jake smiled and shrugged at the same time. "Do I have to answer?" he asked.

"No," Ms. Turner replied. "Your art speaks for itself."

She rummaged in her desk and pulled out a bright red marker. Then, on the back of the canvas, she wrote a large letter "A." Jake was too amazed to speak.

"We'll hang it up next to the SMART Board," Ms. Turner announced. "Who knows, maybe it will inspire your friends, too! Based on what you've accomplished in your painting, I'm really looking forward to reading your Frida Kahlo report."

Jake grinned in response. After meeting Señora Frida and learning about her incredible life, he was really looking forward to writing it!

After school, Jake made his way to the dugout at Franklin Field with heavy footsteps. Another afternoon of warming the bench, alone, watching the rest of his team do the one thing that Jake wanted to do more than anything else in the world. His muscles were practically twitching, he wanted to be on the field so bad. But he'd be back there, Jake knew.

Somebody sat down hard next to Jake, making the wooden bench tremble. Jake looked over in surprise to see Emerson.

"This seat taken?" Emerson asked.

"What are you doing?" Jake asked. "You'd better get out there before Coach shows up. You know how he gets when somebody blows off warm-ups."

"Actually, it turns out I'm benched," Emerson replied.

Jake couldn't hide his shock. "What? Why? What did you do?" he exclaimed.

Emerson ticked the reasons off on his fingers. "Snuck away from the field trip, violated my contract, let down my teachers and my parents and my school," he said. "Just like you. So I got punished just like you."

"I don't understand," Jake said. "You didn't get caught—"

"Yeah, well, I still broke the rules," he said. "It didn't seem, you know, fair. For me to get away with it . . . or for you to take all the blame."

"You confessed?" Jake asked, still astonished.

"Yup," Emerson replied, staring ahead as Sam and Sebastian tossed the ball back and forth. It made a dense, satisfying *thud* as it landed snugly in their gloves.

"I don't really know what to say," Jake told him.

"Promise me something," Emerson said. "Next time I come up with an incredibly dumb idea like running off during a field trip, you'll stop me."

"Only if *you* promise that *you'll* stop me," Jake replied.

"I promise," Emerson said.

"Me, too."

A big smile crossed Jake's face—a real one, for maybe the first time since he'd tripped over the velvet rope at the museum. His punishment—and Emerson's—would be over before too long. His ankle was healing more every day. His team would be in top condition . . . and when it came time to play the Pinehurst Piranhas, Jake would be ready for them.

And *that* was a promise he was determined to keep.

A NOTE FROM THE AUTHOR

When Jack Roosevelt Robinson was born on January 31, 1919, in Cairo, Georgia, no one could have predicted that he would grow up to be a phenomenal baseball player and a civil rights hero. Prejudice against black people made life especially hard and dangerous. Too many white people believed in segregation, the practice of keeping black and white people separate. Restaurants, swimming pools, and even sports were just some of the areas where segregation happened. Racism made life hard in other ways, too. Jackie's parents worked long hours for farm owners who took so much of their earnings that there never seemed to be enough for their kids. When Jackie was young, his father left the family. Jackie's mother knew it was time for a change. All by herself, she moved her family across the country to California.

Jackie was a good student who showed incredible athletic ability even when he was a child.

When he grew up, Jackie decided to go to college, where he played several sports, including football, basketball, track, and baseball. College was also where Jackie met his future wife, Rachel. Before they could get married, though, Jackie was drafted into the army. World War II was underway, and Jackie was proud to serve his country. But even in the army, the ugliness of racism struck again. One night, a bus driver ordered Jackie to move to the back of the bus. When Jackie refused, he was arrested—and put on trial. Fortunately, Jackie was acquitted of all charges.

After Jackie left the army, he started playing baseball for the Negro leagues. But the president of the Brooklyn Dodgers, Branch Rickey, thought it was time for segregation in baseball to end—and he believed Jackie, with his incredible talent and calm temperament, was just the player who could make it happen. Breaking the color line in baseball wasn't easy. Jackie faced constant abuse from fans and players alike. At the same time, Jackie's bravery, dignity, and skill both impressed and inspired thousands of people who flocked to the ballfield just to see him play.

Even after Jackie retired from baseball in 1957, he continued to work for civil rights until his death in 1972. A grateful nation continues to find ways to honor Jackie's life, including awarding him the Presidential Medal of Freedom, inducting him into the Baseball Hall of Fame, and retiring his number, 42, so that no other Major League baseball player could ever wear it.

Jackie didn't just change baseball. He changed the world.

Frida Kahlo was born in Mexico City, Mexico, on July 6, 1907. For much of her life, though, she told people that her birthday was on July 7, 1910, the day the Mexican Revolution started. She loved her country so much that she wanted to share her special day with Mexico!

When Frida was six years old, she became ill with a serious disease called polio. Her recovery took many months, and her experience as a patient inspired her to dream of becoming a doctor. Tragedy struck in 1925 when Frida was seriously injured in a terrible bus accident. While she was lucky to survive, that accident would dramatically change the course of her life. Frida's injuries, which never fully healed, forced her to abandon her plans to become a doctor. To pass the many long hours that she spent recovering, Frida began painting from her bed—and unlocked an incredible artistic talent. Her paintings, which included many self-portraits, combined images from the real world and her imagination to create powerful, haunting artwork. Frida's wardrobe was as vibrant as her paintings. Her gorgeous outfits, in the style of Mexican folkwear, have even been shown in museums.

Frida met Diego Rivera, a famous artist, when she was in high school; they married seven years later, in 1929. Frida and Diego didn't just share tremendous artistic talent; they shared a dream for how the world could be a better place. They also shared strong opinions and passions that led them to have huge fights. Despite their stormy relationship, which led them to divorce and later remarry, Frida never stopped loving Diego.

Frida's injuries from the bus accident got worse as she aged. She endured many surgeries but nothing relieved her pain. Though Frida died in 1954, her incredible artwork continues to inspire people around the world.

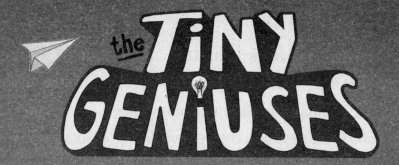

THE TINY GENIUSES ARE LIVE, IN PERSON, AND READY TO HELP!

But can Jake Everdale keep his secret Heroes of History under wraps when the tiny toys are causing BIG problems?